# The Berenstain Bears
## and the
# BIG ROAD RACE

Can Little Red
Keep up the pace?
Can the slowest car
win the race?

PUTT PUTT PUTT

**A FIRST TIME READER**™

# ROAD RACE

## Stan & Jan Berenstain

Random House 🏠 New York

Library of Congress Cataloging-in-Publication Data: Berenstain, Stan. The Berenstain bears and the big road race. (A First time reader) SUMMARY: Papa Bear and his family watch as the little red car competes in a race against the big orange, yellow, green, and blue cars. [1. Automobile racing—Fiction. 2. Bears—Fiction. 3. Color—Fiction. 4. Stories in rhyme [I. Berenstain, Jan. II. Title. III. Title: Berenstain bears and the big road race. IV. Series: Berenstain, Stan. First time reader. PZ8.3.B4493Bfn 1987 [E] 87-4581 ISBN: 0-394-89134-1 (trade); 0-394-99134-6 (lib. bdg.)

18 19 20

Manufactured in the United States of America

Four big cars,

Orange,                                                    Yellow,

Green, and Blue.

"R-r-r!" said Orange,
long and low.

"Vroom!" said Yellow,
ready to go.

"Grrr!" said Green,
big and mean.

"Roar! Roar!"
the blue car said.

Wait! There's one more car!

It was Little Red.
"Putt-putt-putt,"
said Little Red.

When the dust had cleared,
there was Red.
"Putt-putt—cough!"
said Little Red.

Over,

under,

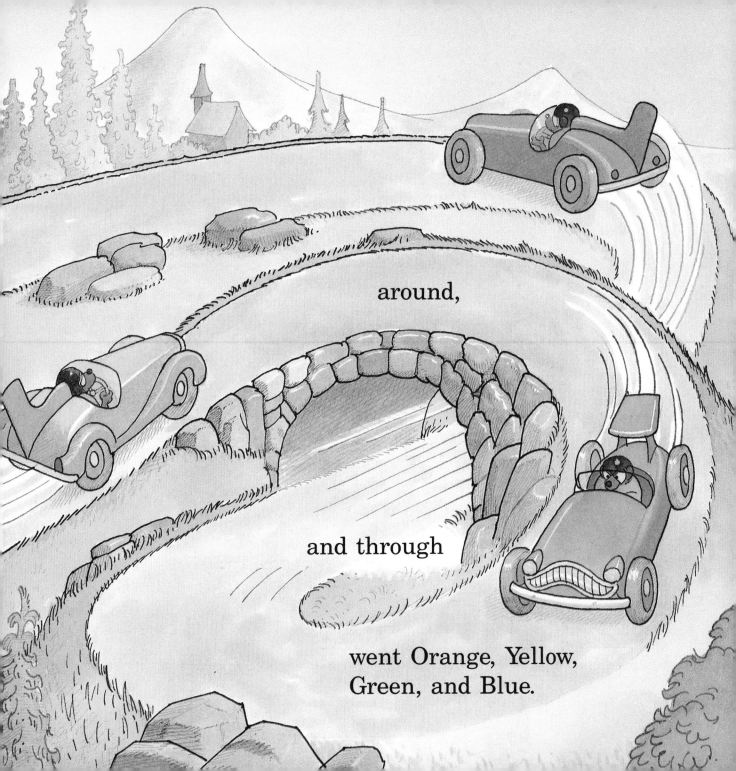

around,

and through

went Orange, Yellow,
Green, and Blue.

Up and down,

down and around,

through the town
and country scene

went Yellow, Orange,
Blue, and Green.

Those other drivers
laughed at Red.
"Ha-ha-ha!"
they all said.
"That Red's a joke.
He's nothing but
an old slowpoke!"

What said Red?
He didn't say grrr
or vroom or roar.
Little Red said
what he said before—

"Putt-putt-putt,
putt-putt-putt-putt!"

There goes Yellow
taking the lead.
Green is second,
putting on speed.
Orange and Blue,
catching up fast.
Where was Red?...

Dead last!

"I cannot lose!"
shouted Yellow,
a very boastful
sort of fellow.
"A first-place finish
is my goal!"
But he was
so busy bragging—

he did not see
a big pothole.

KLUNK

"Ha!" said the others,
roaring past.
Where was Red?
Still behind—
but no longer last.

Who will win
the big road race?
Can these cars
keep up the pace?

Up ahead—
Dead Bear's Curve.
"I won't slow down
for Dead Bear's Curve!"
Orange's driver
was all nerve.

All nerve—
but not much sense.
Orange went
right through the fence.

"It's a two-car race!"
Green's driver said,
forgetting all about
Little Red.
"Putt-putt-putt,"
said Little Red.

The driver of Green
was really mean.
He reached into
the glove compartment.
It was time
for the dirty tricks department.

It wasn't a very
nice thing to do.
But that was that—
the blue car's tires
all went flat.

As he said it
a fast-food store
came into sight.
"Hmmm," said Green.
"Racing gives me
an appetite!"

"I have beaten Orange,
Yellow, and Blue.
As for Red—
nowhere in view.
There's plenty of time
for a little snack—
A burger and fries, please,
in a sack!"

But Red never quit.
He just kept coming.
His putt-putt motor
kept right on humming.
And while Green waited
for his stuff,
Red putted right past.
The fast-food store
wasn't fast enough.

"Look! Look!
It's Little Red!
Hooray! Hooray!"
the bears all said.
"The road race winner
is Little Red!"

PUTT PUTT PUTT PUTT

"Putt-putt-putt,"
said Little Red.